CHRISTMAS
IN OREGON

Sue Carabine

Illustrations by
Shauna Mooney Kawasaki

GIBBS SMITH
TO ENRICH AND INSPIRE HUMANKIND
Salt Lake City | Charleston | Santa Fe | Santa Barbara

13 12 11 10 09   12 11 10 9 8
Text and illustrations © 2002 Gibbs Smith, Publisher

Published by
Gibbs Smith
P.O. Box 667
Layton, Utah 84041

1.800.835.4993 orders
www.gibbs-smith.com

Designed and produced by TTA Design
Printed and bound in China
Gibbs Smith books are printed on either recycled, 100% post-consumer waste, FSC-certified papers or on paper produced from a 100% certified sustainable forest/controlled wood source.

ISBN 13: 978-1-58685-170-5
ISBN 10: 1-58685-170-5

'Twas the night before Christmas
as Santa Claus stood
On Oregon's towering
majestic Mt. Hood.

He breathed in the fresh air,
then said to his deer,
"Do the folks know how lucky
they are to live here?

"Remember last summer
when we all sneaked away
And came here to Oregon
to have fun and play?

"We fished the Rogue River
and had a great time,
But at white-water rafting
you weren't worth a dime!

"You fellows just wanted
to splash and to leap,
But I wanted to swim
and to dive somewhere deep

"Like blue Crater Lake.
If you lads can recall,
'Twas our most favorite spot,
and we all had a ball!

"And now we've returned
to share glad Christmas cheer
In this wonderful state
at this great time of year."

O'er the Columbia River
Nick's bold reindeer soared,
Then followed a trail blazed
two centuries before.

Said Nick at Ft. Clatsop,
"Lads, who left their mark
On this rugged young land?
Why, brave Lewis and Clark!

"They'd forgotten 'twas Christmas,
and knowing they'd miss it,
We'd decided that evening
to pay them a visit!

"Remember the grin
on tough Clark's bearded face
Christmas morn when he opened
his stocking with haste?

"I'd left a gold compass to help
while they roamed—
*Well, we had to make certain
they'd find their way home!*

"And sad Lewis's moccasins
had finally worn through,
So I left him my boots,
which were sturdy and new.

"Well, he kicked up his heels
and yelled, 'Nick, you're a friend!'
Both Lewis and Clark vowed
to endure to the end!

"What courage it took them
to make that decision,
And we honor them now
at their own Exposition!

"Such wonderful memories
we've made in this place.
Let's make more, lads!" cried Nick,
with a mischievous face.

So, they flew from Astoria
straight down the coast
To one of the places
they all loved the most.

The ocean was awesome,
the rugged cliffs tall,
Coos Bay was a harbor
for ships, big and small.

They spied a great lighthouse
(in fact, there were nine),
And Santa called, "Rudolph,
remember that time

"We were here in a storm
and the beacon went out,
And you and your nose
saved a ship, without doubt!"

Then Rudolph said shyly,
nose glowing bright red,
"Look, Nick, down in Salem
the kids are in bed."

Nick smiled, then flew down,
piled gifts 'neath Yuletide trees,
And rose up each chimney
with the greatest of ease.

"Let's challenge this sleigh, lads,
with unique North Pole flying,
And stop by the home of
two boys—Grant and Ryan.

"They'd secretly written
a note, which they sent
To me from a small town
they live in named Bend."

So, the deer made a dash
for the boys' snowbound house,
Where Nick quietly entered
their room like a mouse.

Both sat up in bed,
their eyes big as an owl's.
Grant hugged Ryan tight,
neither let out a howl!

Nick showed them their note.
"Can I help, my young friends?"
"Oh, yes," Ryan stammered,
"our money's all spent!

"And we still didn't find
a nice present for Mom—
Please help us, St. Nick,
to find just the right one."

"A gift that costs nothing?
I must think about this."
Grant said, "What do you give
Mrs. Claus? A big kiss?"

St. Nicholas chuckled,
"Just how did you know
She'd rather have that
than a gift with a bow!

"I think you will find
that your Mom likes that, too,
Along with a card that's
created by you."

They jumped out of bed,
got their crayons and pens.
"Oh, thank you, dear Santa,
you're such a good friend!"

As they flew on to Portland,
Nick said to his deer,
"Those boys got me thinking
that maybe this year

"I'll take back some gifts
from this wonderful place.
Lads, help me decide
'cause there's no time to waste!"

Nick paused, eyeing Cupid
who wistfully said,
"There are frozen fresh berries
of black, blue, and red.

"Do you think Mrs. Claus
would bake us some pies?"
"I'll persuade her," Nick laughed,
with a gleam in his eyes.

"The next thing that comes
to my mind that would please
Is her most favorite snack—
famous Tillamook cheese.

"We'll call at the factory,
taste cool yogurt too,
Buy crawfish from Jake's, lads,
especially for you!"

Said Blitzen, "Let's eat
something different this year,
Like Oregon Ducks . . .
they're quite famous, I hear."

His deer pals turned gleeful
and made quite a scene:
"That's a U of O team,"
Donner laughed, "from Eugene!"

Nick grinned, "Settle down.
The Rose Garden's below—
The Trailblazers asked for
new high-tops, you know.

"After stuffing their stockings,
our load will be light,
Just perfect for sleighing
at Grant's Pass tonight!

"But for now, there are folks
in a shelter this year
Without food and warm clothing—
they'll suffer, I fear.

"Those Pendleton blankets,
the finest I know,
Will protect these good folks
from the sleet and the snow.

"With candies and books
and some bright-colored toys,
We'll fill up the stockings
of sweet girls and boys.

"So pack up the sleigh, boys,
let's be on our way
To bring gladness and warmth
on this bright holiday."

Soon o'er the Blue Mountains,
they paused and gazed down
As soft fragile snowflakes
danced lightly all 'round.

The green fir trees glistened
in mantles of white—
Nick never had seen
a more beautiful sight.

He longingly thought of
each forest and lake,
Then promised his deer,
"Lads, we're making a date